LON

Please renew or return items by the date shown on your receipt

www.hertsdirect.org/libraries

Renewals and enquiries: 0300 123 4049

Textphone for hearing or speech impaired 0300 123 4041

PUFFIN BOOKS

Published by the Penguin Group
Penguin Books Ltd, 80 Strand, London WC2R 0RL, England
Penguin Group (USA) Inc., 375 Hudson Street, New York, New York 10014, USA
Penguin Group (Canada), 90 Eglinton Avenue East, Suite 700, Toronto, Ontario, Canada M4P 2Y3
(a division of Pearson Penguin Canada Inc.)
Penguin Ireland, 25 St Stephen's Green, Dublin 2, Ireland (a division of Penguin Books Ltd)
Penguin Group (Australia), 707 Collins Street, Melbourne, Victoria 3008, Australia
(a division of Pearson Australia Group Pty Ltd)
Penguin Books India Pvt Ltd, 11 Community Centre, Panchsheel Park, New Delhi – 110 017, India
Penguin Group (NZ), 67 Apollo Drive, Rosedale, Auckland 0632, New Zealand
(a division of Pearson New Zealand Ltd)
Penguin Books (South Africa) (Pty) Ltd, Block D, Rosebank Office Park, 181 Jan Smuts Avenue, Parktown
North, Gauteng 2193, South Africa

Penguin Books Ltd, Registered Offices: 80 Strand, London WC2R 0RL, England

puffinbooks.com

First published 2014
001

Written by Poppy Bloom
Illustrations by AMEET Studio Sp. z o.o.
Text and illustrations copyright © AMEET Sp. z o.o., 2014

Produced by AMEET Sp. z o.o. under license from the LEGO Group.

AMEET Sp. z o.o.
Nowe Sady 6, 94-102 Łódź – Poland
ameet@ameet.pl **www.ameet.pl**

LEGO, the LEGO logo and the Brick and Knob configurations
are trademarks of the LEGO Group.
©2014 The LEGO Group.

Set in Bembo.
Printed in Poland by AMEET Sp. z o.o.

British Library Cataloguing in Publication Data
A CIP catalogue record for this book is available from the British Library

ISBN: 978-0-14135-264-0

Item name: LEGO® Friends. Jungle Rescue
Series: LBW
Item number: LBW-104
Batch: 01

Jungle Rescue

Poppy Bloom

Andrea
Star Performer

Mia
Animal Lover

Olivia
Brilliant Inventor

Stephanie
Social Butterfly

Emma
Stylish Designer

Beauty

Matthew
Rescue Base Assistant

Contents

1
Surprise Plan

"What was that?" Mia gasped, sitting up straight as a loud screech echoed through the jungle.

Her friend Stephanie laughed, nervously, "I was just about to ask you the same question, Mia." Stephanie nudged her friend in the arm playfully. "You are our animal expert, after all!"

Their friends, Olivia, Emma and Andrea laughed, too. All five best friends were having lunch in the Jungle Falls Café. That was what Andrea called the comfortable dining area she'd created on a treetop platform near the Hambo River Rescue Base. Olivia's Aunt Sophie and

her husband, Henry, both vets, had helped start
the base, which was located deep in the heart
of the jungle, a long drive over rough dirt
roads from the nearest town. Aunt Sophie had
invited Olivia, Mia, and the others to spend the
summer helping out at the base. Their friend
Matthew had come along, too, since Henry
was his uncle. But then the two vets had been
called away on important business, and
now the five girls and Matthew were in
charge of the whole camp!

Running the rescue base wasn't
easy. But it was one of the
most rewarding
things Mia had
ever done.

"I might be an expert back home in
Heartlake City," she told her friends with
a smile. "But there are animals here in the jungle
that I've never even heard of before!"

Emma flicked a few crumbs off the sleeve of her stylish khaki jacket, then tucked her wavy dark hair behind one ear. "Like that white monkey you were talking about yesterday?" she asked. "It sounded so cute."

Stephanie reached for a jug of juice in the middle of the table. "Did you hear the rest of the story, Emma? Nobody's actually ever seen a pure white monkey in this jungle."

"Not anybody here, anyway," Mia said. "But villagers from different parts of the jungle claim to have seen it. Maggi was telling me some of the local legends about the white monkey." Mia smiled as she thought about the girls' new friend Maggi, who lived in a small village near the rescue camp.

"Yeah, those stories were cool," added Andrea. "Maggi said she once met a guy whose grandmother had been saved from a tiger attack by a white monkey!"

Olivia looked skeptical as she speared a bit of salad with her fork. "His grandmother? That must be one old monkey."

"Or maybe it's a whole species that just hasn't been discovered yet," Mia said. Her heart pounded with excitement at the thought. How cool would it be to discover a brand new animal? That would be like a dream come true for her! Mia loved animals more than anything. She had lots of pets at home, rode her horse as often as she could, and wanted to be a vet when she grew up – just like Dr Sophie.

Andrea grabbed another handful of berries.
"If there's a white monkey out there anywhere,
I'm sure you'll find it," she told Mia.

"Maybe." Mia smiled. "I was thinking
I might go for a hike this afternoon. Maybe I'll
spot some white monkeys then."

"I have a better idea," Stephanie said. "You
can watch for them when we go zip lining
this afternoon!"

"We're going zip lining?" asked Emma.

Stephanie's blue eyes sparkled with
excitement. "Surprise! I arranged it this
morning. Maggi's cousins run the business –
you get to go right over Triangle Gorge!"

"Awesome!" Olivia exclaimed, giving
Stephanie a high five. "I've been wanting to
check out that gorge ever since we got here.
Besides, Matthew has been zip lining lately and
told me it was a blast!"

"Hold on. Zip lining over a gorge?" Andrea put her fork down. "You mean that thing where you go flying through the air a zillion metres above the ground?"

"Right," Stephanie grinned. "Sounds fun, doesn't it?"

Andrea shuddered. "Not to me! I'm afraid of heights."

"Since when?" said Stephanie, sounding skeptical.

Mia was surprised, too. Andrea wasn't exactly the fearful type. She was a born performer

who often sang in front of huge crowds of people without a hint of stage fright. She was also a talented dancer who could back flip and impressed everyone with lots of daring moves in her routines. Besides, there was a small zip line connecting the rescue base's two main buildings. All five girls used it frequently to go back and forth across the Hambo River.

Andrea ran her fingers through her dark hair. The jungle's humid air had made it extra curly. "Since my cousin made me go cliff diving when I was little! It was so scary. I told you guys about it once."

"Oh, of course, I remember," Stephanie said, squeezing her friend's hand kindly. "But don't worry, Andrea. Zip lining across the gorge won't be that different from doing it across the river. And it's much less scary than cliff diving! You'll be fine. We'll all be there to cheer you on."

Just then, Java,
the camp's resident
blue macaw,
fluttered in and
landed on a nearby
railing. Mia turned to
feed the bird a bite of
banana, then turned back
to her friends.

"Wait a minute," she said, feeling confused.
"Andrea, you've never been afraid of hanging out
in Olivia's tree house. That's pretty high up, too!"

Andrea shrugged. "Not compared to zip
lining," she said. "When I've seen it on TV,
the people are way higher than the tree
house. Plus they're hanging from a tiny wire.
And moving really fast."

Mia gulped. She wasn't normally afraid of
a challenge. In fact, she was used to racing

around on her horse, Bella, often going over scary jumps and large fences. But this zip wire didn't sound very safe at all.

"That does sound a little scary," Mia said to her friends. "Maybe I'll stay on the ground and take photos of you guys whizzing by overhead." She patted her camera, which was on the table next to her plate.

"No way." Stephanie waggled a finger at her playfully. "We're all doing it together. No excuses!"

Emma shrugged. "Well, I'm in," she said. "What time are we going, though? And speaking of taking photos, I want to get some shots of the Belly Tree today!"

"You have plenty of time for that," said Stephanie, popping a berry into her mouth. "We don't need to be there for another hour."

"Oh, good." Olivia stood up. "Because I need to take a look at a solar battery that's been losing power."

Mia nodded. "And when Dr Sophie called this morning, I promised her that Matthew and I would take the stitches out of that injured leopard cub."

"OK." Stephanie checked her watch. "Let's just meet at the zip lining place at one o'clock."

"Great," Olivia agreed immediately, and Emma nodded.

Mia exchanged nervous looks with Andrea.

"OK, I guess I'm in," said Mia. "How scary could it be?"

Andrea shivered. "OK. I'm in too."

"Fantastic!" said Stephanie, delighted. She told them all how to get to the zip lining place, then everyone went their separate ways. Mia headed straight for the medical area in the camp's main building. It was a long, low building with a thatched roof. Inside was a well-equipped veterinary lab. At one end of the room were several large pens, tanks, and cages where ill or injured animals could recover.

When she walked in, Mia looked at all of the animals. The leopard cub was batting at the bars of her cage, several snakes were sunning themselves in a tank near the window and the camp's resident monkey, Romeo, was perched on the edge of the snakes' tank, watching them. Nearby, Matthew bent over a cage of tweeting baby birds.

"Hi, Matthew," Mia said. "Ready to take out our little leopard's stitches?"

Matthew straightened up and smiled. "Sure, let's do it!"

It only took a few minutes to hold the small, playful leopard cub steady while Mia carefully removed the stitches. After that, Mia and Matthew tidied up the clinic, fed the animals, and took care of a few other tasks. Running a rescue base was hard work!

Mia was washing her hands at the sink when she saw a flash of white swish past the window. She looked closer, but whatever it was had already disappeared. "I just saw something out there," she told Matthew. "It was white, and about this size." She held up her hands. "Do you think it could've been the white monkey?"

"White monkey?" Matthew smirked. "Let me guess. Has Maggi been filling your head with those old legends again?" He chuckled. "I hate to tell you this, Mia, but

my uncle says nobody has ever found any evidence that the white monkey exists. You probably just saw a cockatoo. Or maybe it was a grey langur monkey – some of those look almost white."

"Oh." Mia glanced out the window again. "Yeah, you're probably right."

Matthew checked his watch. "Oops, I'm late – I told Mum I'd call on the satellite phone and let her know how we're doing out here. I'd better go." After Matthew hurried out, Mia wandered over to the window again. She leaned on the rough wooden sill, peering out into the shadowy depths of the jungle. What she'd seen had been too big to be a cockatoo and too small to be a langur monkey. She was sure of it! Pretty sure, anyway . . .

"There!" Mia blurted out as she saw another flash of white. This time it was no more than a glimpse. Whatever it was was moving through the treetops pretty far away.

But a glimpse was enough for Mia. If there was any chance a white monkey was hanging around the camp, Mia wanted to

see it. Grabbing her camera, she headed for
the door.

Soon she was at the edge of the clearing
where the camp was located. Trails snaked out
into the jungle in every direction.

Mia peered up into the trees. Matthew had
disappeared, and none of Mia's friends were in
sight, either. But Mia barely noticed. She was
focused on that section of the jungle – the spot
where she'd seen the white flash.

One of the trails led that way. Mia took
a few steps along it, then paused and
glanced back at a row of scooters parked in
the clearing. They were there for everyone
at camp to use, and were well suited to
the jungle's rough ground and narrow trails.

"I shouldn't go," Mia said aloud,
remembering that she was supposed to meet
her friends in a little while.

Then she saw another flash of white in the distance. Mia gasped excitedly, hardly believing her eyes. "White monkey, here I come!" she cried, as she jumped onto a scooter and took off down the trail.

2
Zip Zip Hooray!

"Am I late?" Emma called out breathlessly, stopping her scooter and hopping off. Stephanie, Olivia, and Andrea were standing at the base of a long wooden staircase that disappeared into the thick tree canopy overhead.

"Only a little," Andrea said with a smile.

Emma smiled back sheepishly. "Sorry, guys. I was photographing these gorgeous butterflies near the waterfall and lost track of time."

"Don't be silly, it's fine!" Stephanie said. She didn't mind her friend being late at all. Emma was very artistic, and tended to forget everything else when she was caught up in one of her projects.

"Yeah," Olivia added. "Mia isn't here yet."

"Oh, OK then," said Emma. She flopped onto a wooden bench beside the stairway, fanning her face. "Where is Mia, anyway? She can't have forgotten we were supposed to meet up!"

Andrea laughed. "Don't worry, Emma! Anyway, we were actually a little early. So no wonder you and Mia are a little late."

"Yeah," Olivia said. "Steph, Andrea and I left extra time in case we got lost. But we took the boat here, and Andrea never gets lost when she's on the river!"

Stephanie nodded. Since arriving in the jungle, Andrea had discovered a talent for navigating the network of streams snaking off from the Hambo River.

She checked her watch. It was ten past three. "Mia probably got caught up in something at the animal hospital."

"Let's call and find out." Andrea pulled out her mobile phone.

"Our phones don't work here, remember?" Olivia said. "A wireless network requires a base station transceiver to be close enough to provide coverage, and here in the jungle . . ."

"OK, OK!" Andrea hastily shoved her mobile back in her pocket. "I'll take your word for it. No need for a science lesson!"

Olivia smiled and ducked her head. "Sorry."

"It's OK." Stephanie slung an arm around Olivia's shoulders and gave her a big hug. "It's fantastic having our own personal scientist around to explain whatever we need to know! But right now, the only science I'm interested in is gravity, since that's what makes the zip line work. Let's go give it a try!"

"Shouldn't we wait a little longer for Mia?" asked Emma.

Olivia headed for the staircase. "If she's helping with some kind of animal emergency, there's no telling how long she'll be. We might as well start without her — she won't mind."

"Agreed," Stephanie said. "We don't want to get caught in that rainstorm our local friends warned us about when they dropped off our supplies this morning."

"Are you sure we shouldn't wait for her?" Andrea glanced at the road leading towards the camp.

Emma smiled sympathetically. "Still nervous?"

"Maybe a little," Andrea admitted.

Stephanie was already following Olivia up the steps. "Come on already. I'm sure Mia will be here in time for our second run."

All four friends were huffing and puffing by the time they reached the top of the staircase, which led straight up to a roofed platform overlooking the treetops.

"Wow!" Emma exclaimed. "You can see forever from up here!"

Maggi's cousin was waiting for them. He was a young man with curly dark hair and a friendly smile. "Just about!" he agreed. "Welcome to our zip line! Ready for the adventure of a lifetime?"

"Definitely!" Olivia replied. The others nodded.

"Good. First, let's talk about what's going to happen . . ." He went on to explain how the zip line worked, then showed the friends how to put on the harness and hook on to the line. Finally he asked who wanted to go first.

"Me!" Stephanie shouted out quickly. Then she looked around. "Um, unless someone else wants first turn that is?"

"No, be my guest," Andrea said.

"Actually, two of you can go at once," the young man said. "There are two harnesses already set up for you on the zip line!"

"See? You won't have to face your fears alone," Emma told Andrea.

"Good," Andrea said. "In that case, maybe I should get it over with now, before I lose my nerve!"

She and Stephanie got suited up. Soon they were standing at the edge of the platform looking down at the canopy. The jungle floor was hidden from view beneath layers of foliage. Birds fluttered in the treetops, and Stephanie thought she saw a brown monkey swing past.

"Don't forget to watch for Mia's white monkey," she told Andrea. "Maybe that'll distract you from being scared."

"I have a better idea," Emma spoke up. She and Olivia were watching from the back of the platform. "Andrea, if you're feeling nervous, just sing."

"Great idea, Emma!" Stephanie said. She was always impressed by the way Emma seemed to know exactly how to make someone feel better. Andrea loved singing. She always said she forgot everything else whenever she did it.

Andrea's eyes brightened. "That is a good idea," she said. "OK, here goes nothing . . . wheeeeee!"

She leaped off the platform. Stephanie did the same. The two friends flew through the air on the zip line.

"Yaaaaah!" Stephanie yelled excitedly. For a few seconds she was having too much fun to remember to look around.

Then she heard Andrea start singing at the top of her lungs. Glancing over, she saw that she was also clutching the handle tightly and staring down at the ground.

Stephanie grinned, then surveyed the jungle below. She could see everything! The Hambo River glittered wherever it peeked out from behind the trees. The flags of the jungle camp fluttered in the breeze a few kilometers in one direction. In the opposite direction, Stephanie spotted a break in the green expanse of the jungle.

Andrea saw it, too. She stopped singing.
"What's that?" she called across to Stephanie.

Stephanie had researched every detail about
the jungle camp before she left, and knew the
answer right away. "That must be the Triangle
Gorge," she called back. "It's called that because
it's narrow on one end and super wide on the
other – which means it's shaped sort of a like
a huge, long triangle."

A moment later the girls were crossing the
narrow end of the gorge. Even Stephanie, who
wasn't afraid of heights at all, gasped and held
on a little tighter as she looked down into the
dizzying depths. The gorge was so deep that
she could barely see the river snaking along
at the very bottom.

"Look, there's the bridge," she called to
Andrea, pointing. "Dr Sophie says it's the only
way across unless you hike all the way around."

But when she looked over, Andrea's eyes were closed tight. "Let me know when we're back over the trees," Andrea exclaimed. "Looking at that gorge reminds me too much of cliff diving!"

Seconds later, they were back over the jungle and the gorge had disappeared behind them. "OK, you're safe," Stephanie said. "You can look again."

"Good." Andrea opened her eyes and grinned. "Because this is kind of fun. Look – monkeys!"

Stephanie looked at where her friend was pointing. A whole family of macaques were playing in the treetops.

"No white monkeys, though," she laughed, as she and Andrea zipped past the monkeys.

When they landed, another of Maggi's cousins was waiting for them. "How was it?" he asked with a smile.

"Great," Stephanie said breathlessly. Then she glanced over at Andrea. "Want to go again, or was it too scary?"

Andrea grinned. "It was definitely scary. But definitely fun, too. Let's go again!"

Glancing up, they saw Emma and Olivia zipping past on the lines. Emma was too busy screaming to notice them, but Olivia spotted them and waved. A second later both girls joined Andrea and Stephanie.

All the girls jumped into an off-road vehicle and drove back towards the starting platform, following signs marking the way.

"I hope Mia's there when we get back," Stephanie said. "She won't want to miss this!"

But Mia hadn't arrived when they reached the starting platform. By the time the girls returned for their third go, Stephanie was starting to worry.

"I hope Mia didn't get lost," she said, checking her watch.

Olivia shrugged. "I doubt it. She probably felt bad about leaving Matthew to take care of all the animals by himself all afternoon and decided to stay!"

"Yeah," Andrea agreed. "She didn't seem very excited about zip lining."

"Come on, let's have one more turn." Emma urged. "If Mia's still not here by then, we'll head back to camp and see what's up."

3

White Monkey Trail

"Here, monkey monkey monkey," Mia sang
softly, clutching the handlebars of her scooter
as she peered into the treetops. She'd spent the
past hour chasing occasional flashes of white
moving through the trees ahead of her. But
now she hadn't seen the monkey – if that was
really what she'd been following – for at least
fifteen minutes. Had she lost the trail?

She started her scooter and drove along
the dirt path, still scanning the canopy. After
a moment, the trees thinned out, and she came
to an open area covered in grass.

"Oh, wow!" she said, as she saw the ground drop away on the far side of the open area. "I guess this must be the gorge."

Mia stopped the scooter and grabbed her camera out of its storage compartment. She'd heard about Triangle Gorge, but she hadn't seen it for herself yet. It was even bigger than she'd expected, stretching far into the distance.

She snapped a few photos. Then, squinting against the afternoon sun, Mia glanced across. The gorge wasn't very wide at this end – probably less than the width of the riding arena back at Heartlake Stables.

Just then, something moved in

the trees on the opposite bank. Mia gasped.
Was that a long, white tail whipping around?

Her heart pounded with excitement.
It was the white monkey – she was sure of it!
But how had it made its way across the gorge?
Even here at the narrow end, the gorge was far
too wide for a monkey – or anything else –
to jump!

Glancing around, she caught a glimpse of
sun shining on metal. The bridge! It was less
than half a kilometre away.

Rushing back to her scooter, Mia put it in
gear and headed for the bridge. It was a little
scary riding across – she didn't dare look down.
But the bridge was wide enough for a truck
to cross and felt very sturdy beneath her
tyres. Mia focused on the jungle ahead where
the white monkey waited.

"Eep!" Mia squeaked, as her scooter bounced over a rough patch of ground.

At least half an hour had passed since she'd crossed the bridge, and Mia had only seen a few flashes of white in the treetops that whole time. The jungle was even wilder on this side of the gorge, the foliage thicker and the trails much narrower and more winding than those closer to camp. It was a good thing the all-terrain scooter could handle just about any kind of track, because the white monkey was leading her on one wild journey! *I just hope I can find my way back to camp*, Mia thought, anxiously.

Slowing the scooter, she glanced behind her. With a sigh of relief, she saw that the scooter was leaving a clear track in the dirt path. She could follow the tyre marks back to the bridge.

But first, she had to find that monkey . . .

As she turned around, there was another flash of white just ahead. "A-ha!" Mia muttered. "Gotcha!"

She gunned the scooter's motor, keeping her gaze fixed on the treetops. A moment later, she found herself in a large, rocky clearing, dotted with wildflowers and tufts of tall grass. In the centre was a scraggly tree – and perched on one bare branch was a huge, magnificent cockatoo!

Mia stopped the scooter and stared at the big white bird, her heart sinking. The cockatoo ignored her, preening its tail feathers. Was that what she'd been following all this time?

"No way," she murmured. She knew what a cockatoo looked like – there were lots of them

in the jungle around the camp. Mia had been so certain this was something else . . .

She shook her head, imagining what her friends would say when they heard. Emma would be sympathetic, Andrea would probably laugh and make a joke, Olivia would launch into a lecture about how unlikely it was that a white monkey could exist in the area without being identified before now, and Stephanie would want to take her mind off of it by rushing her off to the next activity she'd planned for the group. An activity like . . .

"Zip lining!" Mia exclaimed aloud. "Oh my gosh – I totally forgot!"

She checked her watch. It was nearly three o'clock! Her friends were probably frantic with worry by now, wondering where she was and why she'd never showed up to meet them at one o'clock.

Revving the scooter so
loudly that the cockatoo
squawked and flew off,
Mia turned and sped
back down the trail.
Sure enough, her tracks
were easy to follow even in the dim sunlight
filtering through the jungle canopy. But
after just a few minutes, the scooter's engine
spluttered and died.

Glancing at the fuel gauge, Mia winced.
It was empty!

"Oh, man," she muttered, climbing off of
the scooter and glancing down the trail. It was
going to be a long walk back to camp. "Better
get going," she told herself with a sigh. After
one last look at the scooter, she hurried off.

4
Missing Mia

"Are you sure you haven't seen her?"
Stephanie asked Matthew.

Matthew shrugged. "Sorry, girls. I haven't
seen Mia since we took out those stitches
earlier. I've been busy in the communications
station, so that's no surprise. Why don't you
take another look around camp before
you panic?"

"Good idea." Stephanie glanced at her
friends. "Let's go find her."

Mia wasn't in the vet station or the Jungle
Falls Café. She wasn't down by the river,

either, or at the outdoor pens where the larger
animals stayed. Emma even ran to check
the native village where Maggi lived, but
nobody there had seen Mia, either.

"This is bad," Stephanie said. "Where could
Mia be? What if she's in trouble?"

Emma looked anxious. "Maybe she got lost on the way to the zip lining place."

"We should use the satellite phone to call the bigger village," Olivia said.

Andrea shook her head. "It would take a long time for anyone to get here and start looking. It could be dark by then!"

"Andrea's right," Stephanie agreed. "We have to find her ourselves!"

"But how?" Olivia sounded worried. "We have no idea where she went. And the jungle is huge!"

Just then Matthew hurried to join them. "Did you find her?" he asked.

"No," Emma said. "We're trying to figure out where to look next."

"You were the last person to see her," Stephanie told Matthew. "Did she say anything that could give us a clue about where she went?"

"Not really." Then Matthew snapped his fingers. "Wait, I remember something. She was all excited because she thought she'd spotted a white monkey through the clinic window." He gave the friends a worried look. "I told her there was no such thing, but you know how she is."

The friends exchanged a look. "She saw the white monkey?" Stephanie asked.

"She saw something," Matthew said, shrugging a little. "But probably just a bird or something like that."

Olivia looked thoughtful. "If Mia saw the white monkey – or thought she did – I bet she tried to get a better look. She could be out in the jungle searching for it."

"What if she got lost?" Emma said. "It'll be dark in a few hours!"

"We need to find her!" Andrea exclaimed.

Olivia nodded. "But first, we need a plan."

She, Emma, and Andrea all turned to stare at Stephanie. "Well?" Andrea asked her. "You're the party planner. How about planning a search party?"

Stephanie knew her friends were right – they needed a plan. And Stephanie was an expert planner.

"OK," she said, her mind racing with ideas. "First we need to figure out which direction she went — and whether she was on foot or took one of the vehicles. We already know she didn't borrow the Jeep or the Rescue Boat, since we had those with us." She pointed at Andrea. "Go find out if she took the Jungle Boat . . . And Olivia, you check to see if any of the scooters are missing."

Both girls nodded and raced off. "What do we do?" Emma asked.

"Wait," Stephanie replied. "We can't start checking for footprints or whatever until we know whether she's on foot."

Moments later, Andrea returned. "Both boats are where they belong," she reported breathlessly. "The helicopter's still there, too, so she didn't take that, either."

55

At that moment Olivia rushed up, red-faced and breathless. "She took a scooter," she said. "At least I'm pretty sure she did. One is gone, and there are tracks leading out into the jungle behind the animal hospital."

"She must have gone to look for the white monkey she saw out there," Emma said.

"Or *thought* she saw," Olivia corrected. "The white monkey probably isn't even real."

"Who knows?" Stephanie sighed, walking toward the parking area where they'd left the Rescue Jeep. "Let's get out there and find her!"

5

Homeward Trail

"Wow," Mia whispered, pausing to stare at a row of enormous flying bats hanging upside down in a tree overhead. She'd seen plenty of bats zipping through the darkened skies near camp at night, but this was the first time she'd spotted any during daylight hours.

They looked even bigger up close! For a second she was glad her scooter had run out of fuel. If she'd been driving, she might have been moving too fast to take a second look at the dark shapes hanging high in the tree.

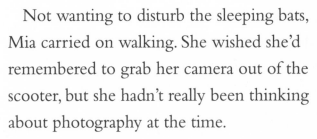

Mia had been walking for what felt like ages, though it had probably only been about half an hour since she'd abandoned the scooter. In that time, she'd seen more wildlife than she'd ever imagined possible. She'd thought there were a lot of interesting animals, birds, and insects near the camp. But out here, far from the sights and sounds of humans, the jungle was alive with animals!

Not wanting to disturb the sleeping bats, Mia carried on walking. She wished she'd remembered to grab her camera out of the scooter, but she hadn't really been thinking about photography at the time.

"Oh well," she told herself as she trudged along. "I'll just have to remember everything I see. My friends will want to hear all about it when I get back."

She paused again
as a pretty orange and
black butterfly fluttered past.
It looked like a Tiger Butterfly.
She wished Olivia was there – she'd
probably know for sure.

In fact, Mia wished *all* of her friends were
with her. Maybe being stranded so far out in
the jungle wouldn't seem so scary with them
around. Stephanie would surely have a rock-
solid plan to get home before dark. Emma
would be pointing out the loveliest views
to distract them from their worries. Andrea
would sing songs or crack jokes to keep them
all in good spirits as they walked. Come to
think of it, they probably wouldn't have to
walk, since Olivia might have been able to rig
up some way to turn her solar powered watch
into an energy source for the scooter . . .

Mia was smiling at that thought when she reached a rocky section of the trail.

The scooter's tyre tracks disappeared in the stones and tree roots, and Mia had a moment of panic before she spotted the tracks emerging on the far side of the rocky area.

"Phew!" she said aloud, causing a bird to dart out of the underbrush nearby. "I don't know what I'd do if I didn't have the tracks to follow back to camp." She glanced around at the trees surrounding her. "I'd be totally lost and helpless out here."

Her heart skittered with anxiety. Then she looked up at the sun peeking down at her through breaks in the canopy. It had moved across the sky since she'd set out, heading towards the far horizon. Mia smiled as she realized what that meant.

Actually, I wouldn't be helpless, she thought. *I could*

use the position of the sun to figure out which
way to walk to get to the gorge. And once
I got across the bridge, I could definitely figure
out the trail back to camp!

That thought made her feel better.
She walked faster, keeping one eye on the tyre
tracks and the other on the scenery.

After a few minutes she heard loud chattering
in the treetops. Pausing again, she peered up and
saw a family of monkeys just overhead.

"Gibbons," she murmured. She'd spotted a few
of the shy creatures near camp, but they'd always
disappeared as soon as they spotted people.

But these gibbons didn't even seem to notice
her standing there. They swung gracefully
through the trees, using their long arms and legs
to grab branches. A tiny baby clung to one of
the adults, and two younger monkeys shoved at
each other playfully, chattering and squawking.

Mia grinned as another adult monkey swung over and chattered irritably at one of the youngsters. She never got tired of watching animals in their natural habitat, whether it was squirrels in her backyard in Heartlake City or these exotic monkeys in the jungle.

I only wish I could see the white monkey out here, she thought with a sigh.

Once the gibbon family had moved out of view, she started walking again. After a moment, the dim light beneath the canopy dimmed even more. Glancing up, Mia saw dark clouds filling the sky.

"Uh oh," she muttered.

Moments later, the first fat raindrops found their way through the leaves, spattering on the dry dirt of the trail. Mia had been in the jungle long enough to know that the drizzle was likely to turn into a downpour – and fast. She spun around, trying to spot anything that she could use as shelter.

Luckily, there was great mound of rocks just a short distance ahead, with what looked like a cave at their base. Mia sprinted towards them as fast as she could, but she was still drenched by the time she reached them and ducked into the small cave for shelter.

"Wow," she exclaimed breathlessly, brushing as much of the moisture off of herself as she could. "When it rains, it pours. At least it does out here in the jungle!"

She stared out at the rain, which was pouring down like a wet curtain outside, forming little rivers in the dirt and making the leaves dance. A breeze blew cold spray into the cave and Mia huddled back against the rock wall behind her. She could only hope that if some wild animal used this cave as its shelter, it wouldn't return and find her there before the rain stopped!

She also hoped the rain would end soon, too, or she'd never make it back to camp before dark.

6

Stormy Skies

"Put it in four wheel drive!" Olivia shouted in Stephanie's ear, leaning forward from the backseat of the Rescue Jeep.

"It *is* in four wheel drive." The rain was pouring heavily down the windscreen. It was falling from the sky in buckets and making it impossible for the friends to see much beyond the bonnet.

Emma clutched the passenger side armrest, looking nervous. "Maybe we should stop and wait it out," she suggested.

"Good idea," Stephanie said. "I just want to

pull over to the side in case anyone else comes
by and – oh, no!"

Suddenly, the Jeep's tyres hit a patch of thick,
slick mud, and Stephanie felt the steering
wheel being yanked out of her grip as if it
were alive. The whole vehicle skidded sideways.

"Stop! We're sliding!" Andrea cried.

"I know!" Stephanie grabbed the wheel,
steering into the skid as her mum had taught her.

But it was too late. The car lurched to a stop, tilted slightly sideways half on and half off the trail and the engine cut out.

"Whoa," Andrea exclaimed. "Are we stuck?"

"Let me see." Stephanie started the engine again and cautiously pushed down on the accelerator pedal. The wheels spun, sending mud flying everywhere, and the engine made an unsettling whining sound.

"We're definitely stuck," Olivia said matter-of-factly. "Ease up on the accelerator, Steph.

Otherwise you'll just dig it in deeper."

Stephanie did as she was told and turned off the engine. "Now what?" Emma asked.

"We'll have to get it unstuck," Stephanie said, her mind already jumping back into planning mode. "We might be able to put a jacket or something beneath the tyres, or –"

"We can't do anything until this rain lets up," Olivia interrupted, staring out of the window. "We'll have to wait it out."

Stephanie opened her mouth to argue. They couldn't just sit around waiting for the rain to stop – not when Mia was out there somewhere!

Then she realized Olivia was right. Even if they went out right that minute and got drenched freeing the vehicle, it was too dangerous to drive any further until the storm was over.

"Fine," she said with a sigh. "Let's just hope it passes soon."

It seemed to take forever, but the rain finally slowed to a drizzle and stopped. The girls climbed out.

"Watch out for the puddles," Emma said, stepping gingerly around a spot of mud.

"Never mind that," Stephanie said, already peering at the front tyres. "Let's get this thing unstuck!"

"How?" Andrea glanced at Olivia. "It looks pretty bad."

Olivia was already grabbing sticks and dried palm leaves from the edge of the trail. "Gather more dry stuff to wedge under the tyres!" she instructed. "While we're doing that, Steph, get back in and turn the wheel back and forth a few times to clear space around the tyres, too."

The others did as she said. Soon, there were mats of leaves and branches in front of each muddy tyre.

"Now what?" Emma asked. "Should we get back in the Jeep?"

"No – just Stephanie!" Olivia instructed. "We don't want to weigh it down anymore than we have to." She explained to Stephanie how to accelerate slowly to allow the muddy tyres to find some grip.

"It'll work," Olivia said, sounding confident as everyone stood back from the Jeep. Then she cupped her hands around her mouth.

"Go ahead and give it a try!" she called
to Stephanie.

Stephanie gave her a thumbs-up out the
open window. Then she turned on the engine.
She held her breath as she pressed carefully on
the accelerator.

The tyres skidded, and for a second,
Stephanie was afraid it wasn't working.
Then she felt the tyres grab the mats packed
in front of them.

The vehicle started
moving.

"Yes!" Stephanie cried, giving the Jeep
a little more acceleration. It spurted forward,
almost stopped, then moved again. Seconds
later, it was back on solid ground.

"You did it!" Andrea whooped, dancing
towards the vehicle, pumping her fist in the air.
"Awesome driving, Steph!"

"Yeah," Emma added. "And great job
figuring out what to do, Olivia."

"Thanks," Stephanie said, putting the vehicle in neutral as her friends climbed back in. "But hurry – we've got to keep looking for Mia."

Andrea glanced at the trail ahead. "Oh no! The tyre tracks have disappeared!"

Stephanie's heart sank as she realized her friend was right. The rain had washed away every trace of Mia's tracks.

"Never mind," she said, trying to sound confident. "We know which way they

were leading. We can just follow this trail for now. If we come to a fork, we'll decide what to do then."

As she drove on, Stephanie did her best to avoid the bigger puddles and muddy spots. It wasn't easy. Especially since the trail got narrower the further they went from camp. Luckily they didn't get stuck again – but their luck soon ran out when they rounded a curve and saw the trail disappear into a large ditch.

"Whoa," Emma said as Stephanie slammed on the brakes. "What's that?"

Stephanie peered out the muddy windshield. "Looks like the storm washed out the road."

They all climbed out for a better look. "Even an all-terrain vehicle isn't getting through *that*," Olivia said.

Stephanie nodded slowly. "We'll have to turn back."

"But we'll lose Mia's trail!" Emma exclaimed.

"We already lost it," Andrea pointed out.
"We might as well go back and see if Matthew
has heard from her."

Emma brightened. "Maybe she's back by
now! She might have found her way home
while we were out here looking for her."

"True," Olivia said. "Without mobile phone
service, they'd have no way to let us know."

Suddenly, Andrea gripped Stephanie's arm
so hard she yelped. "Ssh! Look!" Andrea hissed,
pointing across the ditch.

Stephanie, Olivia, and Emma looked where
Andrea was pointing. Stephanie's eyes widened
as she saw an enormous orange-and-black
striped creature slipping through the trees
just a few metres away on the far side of
the ditch.

"A tiger!" she whispered in awe.

She held her breath as the majestic animal
paused and glanced at them with intense
amber eyes. After a long moment, the tiger

turned and continued on its way, quickly
vanishing into the trees.

Nobody spoke for a moment. Finally, Emma
let out her breath in a whoosh.

"Wow," she said. "That was *amazing*. And
a little scary."

"Yeah." Olivia bit her lip. "Mia would have
loved it."

Stephanie traded a look with the others.
She could tell they were thinking the same

thing she was – Mia might still be out there somewhere. And while tigers were beautiful, they could also be dangerous. So could lots of other creatures in the jungle.

"Come on," she said, turning and hurrying back to the vehicle. "We'd better get going."

It was a slow, difficult journey back to camp. The roads and trails were full of puddles and potholes after the storm, and a couple of times Stephanie had to wrestle with the steering wheel to keep the vehicle from sliding into more mud.

But finally the camp's tall wooden gate came into view. As the girls climbed out of the Jeep, Matthew hurried out to meet them.

"Did you find Mia?" he called out.

Stephanie gulped as she realized what the question meant. "She didn't come back?" she asked.

"No," said Matthew worriedly. "And nobody will be able to make it out from town to help us find her. I called on the satellite phone, and they said part of the road just washed out in a flash flood."

Stephanie glanced up. The sky was now a clear blue, but the sun's trek towards the far horizon was well underway.

"We'd better figure out a new plan," she said. "It'll be dark pretty soon, and Mia needs us."

"What kind of plan?" Emma asked.

Stephanie felt a twinge of anxiety as her three friends turned to gaze at her hopefully. "I don't know yet," she said. "But I'll think of something!"

7

Detours and Decisions

The storm was over, and the hot afternoon sun made the droplets clinging to every leaf and flower petal glitter like jewels. But Mia couldn't enjoy the beauty that surrounded her. Night would fall soon, and as much as Mia loved wildlife, she didn't relish the thought of being out there with the creatures that crept out after dark.

Her mind had been filled with such worry from the moment the storm had ended and she'd realized that the pounding rain had completely obliterated the scooter's tyre tracks.

She could follow the position of the sun for now, but as soon as it set, she'd have no idea which direction to go. She had to move fast if she didn't want to be stranded overnight.

Reaching another fork in the trail, Mia stopped and squinted up at a patch of sky visible through the treetops. It was hard to keep going the right way when the trails twisted and turned so much, but she didn't dare leave them, either. Who knew what could be out there? She could stumble into anything – a patch of quicksand, a tangle of thorny brambles or even a nest of stinging insects!

"This way," she muttered, glancing down the left hand trail. "I think."

She started off down the new fork, skirting a large muddy puddle in the middle. The path meandered downhill, and after a moment Mia heard the sound of splashing water. Biting her lip, she paused. She hadn't crossed any part of the Hambo River on her way here – well, except for the one at the bottom of Triangle Gorge, of course – and she hadn't seen any waterfalls, either. So what was she hearing up ahead?

"Only one way to find out," she whispered, stepping forward again.

A moment later she emerged into a large clearing. Most of it was taken up by a muddy pond – and playing in the water was an entire family of black bears!

Mia inhaled sharply, stepping back as quickly and quietly as she could into the shelter of the trees. The vets at the camp had warned the girls about this species of bear. Unlike the gentle pandas they sometimes saw near camp, she had heard that these black bears didn't like humans very much.

Still, Mia couldn't resist pausing to watch the bear family. Several cubs were tumbling around in the shallows, splashing and leaping on each other with playful grunts and squeals. Both parents were lounging nearby, enjoying the cool water.

Suddenly a bird let out a squawk somewhere in the trees behind Mia, making her jump. One of the adult bears turned its head towards her, and Mia took several quick steps backwards. Then she turned and raced away, her heart pounding.

She didn't slow down until she was sure the bears weren't following her. Then she stopped to catch her breath, leaning against the rough bark of a tree. Usually she loved having animals around, but at the moment, every flash of movement seemed scary. This time it had been bears – what if she stumbled across a pack of wild dogs next? Or a deadly viper? Or a hungry tiger?

Mia's eyes filled with tears as she thought more and more about what a scary situation she was in. What was she going to do?

We can figure it out, a little voice in her head said. The voice sounded

a lot like Olivia's – that was one of her
favourite sayings, and it actually made Mia feel
a tiny bit braver.

Mia focused on her friend. What would
Olivia suggest if she were here?

"She'd tell me to stop and think," Mia
whispered. "And Stephanie would already be
coming up with a plan of action, and Andrea
would be cheering me on, and then Emma
would put her arm around me and tell me
everything was going to be OK."

Thinking about her friends made her smile.
If they were here with her, she wouldn't feel
scared at all. And they were here with her –
in her heart and mind at least, if not in person.
All Mia had to do was remember that, and
maybe everything really *would* be OK.

She swallowed hard and realized that her
throat felt dry and scratchy. She desperately

needed a drink of water. Glancing over her shoulder, she thought about the pond.

"But that water wouldn't be safe to drink even if the bears weren't around," she whispered to herself.

Glancing around, she saw sunlight sparkling off a little pool of water caught in a large leaf nearby.

Mia smiled. "Rainwater," she said. "That should be safe."

She carefully tipped the leaf so the cool water ran into her mouth. Then she looked around for more. Thanks to the storm, there were plenty of leaves that still held some rainwater, and soon her thirst was gone.

Feeling more hopeful than before, Mia set off again, choosing another trail that skirted well around the pond where the bears were. The trail led upward over a rocky slope,

then downhill again.
After a while the
trees thinned out
ahead, and Mia
slowed, hoping
she hadn't
misjudged and
circled back
towards that pond.

Creeping forward,
she peered out – and smiled
with relief. It wasn't the pond lying before her.
It was the gorge!

"Thank goodness," she murmured, stepping
out of the trees into the warm afternoon
sunshine. The gorge was several kilometres from
camp, but the trails on the far side were wide
and smooth, and Mia was pretty sure she knew
the way. She'd easily make it back before dark.

Or would she? When she glanced around for
the bridge, it was nowhere in sight.

"Huh?" she said, feeling confused.

She stepped forward, wondering if the bright
sun was blinding her. But when she took
a closer look at the gorge, her heart sank as she
realized something. It was wider here than it
was near the bridge. Much wider.

Oh, no. She was nowhere near the spot
where she'd crossed before! She had to be
close to the far end of the gorge, the wide
part of the triangle. That was really far from
the bridge!

For a moment Mia felt like crying again.
But she shook it off. At least she wasn't totally
lost. She glanced one way and then the other,
trying to remember how long the gorge
was. Dr Henry and Dr Sophie had told her,
but Mia had been more interested in asking

questions about the local wildlife and hadn't really been paying attention to the other stuff. If only Olivia was here – she'd remember for sure! She loved numbers and statistics and things like that.

But Olivia wasn't there, which meant Mia had to work this out for herself. She could walk east until she came to the bridge, which was almost certainly at least 12 kilometres away at the narrow end. Then she would have to walk across the bridge, which could be pretty scary – it was meant for vehicles, and the bottom was mesh. It would be hard to avoid looking down into the terrifying depths beneath her feet!

Then again, she could go the other way, towards the wide end of the triangle, and hike all the way around it. Once she made it to the other side, all she'd have to do was follow the edge of the gorge until she reached the area near camp.

The second option sounded better to her. Either way, she was still likely to be out in the jungle after dark. But at least this way she wouldn't be stuck trying to cross that bridge by moonlight!

And at least I won't get lost with the gorge right there, Mia told herself as she set off to the west. *Maybe once it gets dark I can figure out a way to build a fire signal.* She grimaced as her shoe squished in a patch of deep mud. *If I can find any wood that's dry enough, that is . . .*

She kept walking, with the gorge on her right and the jungle on her left. Suddenly Mia caught a glimpse of movement in the trees. She glanced that way, hoping it was a bird or something instead of a tiger or a bear. A flash of white was just disappearing into some heavy brush.

Her heart thumped. Was it the white monkey?

Then Mia sighed. "Forget it," she muttered. This wasn't the time to think about spotting the mythical monkey. She had to focus on getting home.

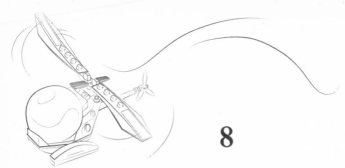

8

Rescue Mission!

"Are you sure you know how to fly this thing?" Matthew looked worried as he watched Stephanie and her friends climb into the helicopter that belonged to the camp.

"Absolutely," Stephanie replied, settling herself in the captain's seat. "I've flown just about everything they have at the Heartlake City Flight School."

"She really has," Emma assured him.

Matthew glanced over his shoulder towards the camp. "Maybe we should call the village again. They might be able to get here by now."

"We'll be fine," Andrea told him. "Besides, we can't wait."

Olivia nodded. "It'll be dark in a few hours, and we need to find Mia."

Andrea grinned. "Are you sure you don't want to come with us?"

Matthew took a step backwards. "That's OK, I'd better stay here in case Mia comes back while you're gone," he said. "Be careful, OK?"

"We promise." Stephanie reached for the controls. "Everyone strapped in?" she asked her friends. "Good. Then let's get up there!"

Soon the helicopter was lifting off into the sky. All traces of the storm had disappeared, and only a few fluffy white clouds drifted overhead.

"It's a good thing you learned how to fly a helicopter at the flight school," Olivia said. "Otherwise we'd never be able to find Mia in time."

"We might not find her this way, either." Andrea had her face pressed to the passenger side window. She was too worried about Mia to think about being scared of heights, and besides, she trusted Stephanie's expert flying skills. "It's going to be hard to see anything through these trees."

"Mia's smart." Stephanie adjusted the controls, then glanced at the ground. "If she's

lost out there somewhere, she's probably
already got a signal fire going."

Olivia raised one eyebrow. "After that rain?
She'll never be able to find enough dry wood.
And while wet wood will eventually dry out
enough to burn if exposed to high enough
temperatures, it's not like Mia's got a blowtorch
in her pocket, or –"

"OK, OK, I know," said Stephanie, trying
not to panic. "So then maybe she's spelled out
HELP with coconuts or something. Anyway,
we'll find her!"

Emma nodded. "We have to!"

After that, everyone stopped talking for
a while. Stephanie flew as low over the jungle
as she could, heading in the direction Mia's tyre
tracks had been going before they'd lost the trail.

"There's the gorge," Andrea commented as
they passed over the giant ravine.

Stephanie squinted as the glint of sunlight on metal caught her eye. "Let's check down by the bridge," she suggested, steering that way. "She must have crossed there – maybe she's found her way back to it by now."

She swooped down even lower, setting the top branches of nearby trees dancing in the wind created by the helicopter's blades. All four friends peered out, searching the area for any glimpse of their friend.

Finally Stephanie sighed and grabbed the controls to climb higher.

"Guess Mia's not down there," she said, trying to sound upbeat. "Let's keep going – and keep looking."

At that moment, Mia paused and turned around, hearing a strange buzzing sound from far behind her. With the sun at her back, it was easy to see a long way in the now clear blue sky.

Something was flying up there, so far away it
was little more than a speck. But she heard the
faint noise of an engine.

"It's a helicopter!" she whispered, as she saw
the speck rise through the air and turn towards
the jungle. She gasped. "A helicopter!" she
cried more loudly. "Hey, over here!"

Mia jumped up and down, whistling
and yelling at the top of her lungs. But the
helicopter circled the narrow end of the gorge
once more, then flew off over the treetops,
deeper into the jungle.

Mia stopped jumping, sadly. They hadn't seen
her. No wonder – if the helicopter looked like

a speck to her at
this distance, she
wouldn't be visible
to the people
inside at all.

Still, she took another few steps in that
direction, wondering if she was making
a mistake by heading for the wide end of
the triangle. Maybe she should hike back
towards the bridge at the narrow end after
all – especially if that was where people were
looking for her . . .

"No," Mia told herself firmly. She'd already
gone so far towards the wide end – she
couldn't turn back now, or she'd never reach
the other side of the gorge before nightfall. As
she turned and walked briskly west, she
saw something move in the jungle nearby.
Something quick – and white.

This time she couldn't resist stopping and
squinting at it. What if it really was the white
monkey? No matter which direction she
walked, Mia wouldn't get back to camp before
dark anyway; why not at least try to catch

a glimpse of the creature she'd come out here to see?

She took a few steps towards the jungle. "No," she whispered, stopping just short of the tree line. "Don't be stupid. It's probably just another cockatoo. There's no such thing as a white monkey."

She scanned the trees once more, then turned away. As she did so, she stepped aside to avoid another patch of mud.

Then she saw something in the mud and stopped short with a gasp. It was a paw print – a monkey's print! She was sure of it.

Her heart thumped as she leaned closer, studying the imprint in the mud. Nothing else in the jungle would leave a print like that. There had definitely been a monkey there recently.

"That doesn't mean it was a white monkey," Mia whispered.

She bit her lip, glancing from the jungle to the gorge and back again. She still had a long hike ahead of her, but she'd been counting on making it around the wide end of the gorge to the camp side before dark. If she stopped to search for white monkeys, she might not make it that far.

Out of the corner of her eye, Mia caught another flash of white. Spinning around, she was just in time to see a long, white tail whipping out of sight behind a cluster of leaves.

Had that been the white monkey? Mia wasn't sure. It could have been a grey langur monkey with a particularly pale tail. Or maybe heat and hunger and exhaustion were getting to Mia's head, and

107

it hadn't been a tail at all. It could have been
a cockatoo's extra long feather. Or even a light
coloured tree snake.

But it hadn't really looked like any of those
things. It had looked like a white monkey –
maybe. At least it had looked enough like one
that Mia couldn't stand to move on without
checking it out.

"I'm probably making a big mistake," she
muttered as she turned and stepped into
the trees.

Still, she kept going, scanning the treetops.
There! Another flash of white moved to her
left. She turned and hurried that way.

The white monkey – if that was what it
was – seemed to be swinging from tree to tree
along the edge of the forest, heading east. That
made Mia feel uneasy – if she followed it, she'd
be heading back the way she'd come.

At least it seemed to be staying near
the gorge. If this turned out to be another
wild goose chase – or a wild cockatoo chase,
as the case may be – Mia wasn't going to get
lost again. Besides, maybe it had been a mistake
to keep walking away from that helicopter
she'd spotted . . .

"Here, monkey monkey monkey," she called
out softly, trying not to worry as she caught
another glimpse of white just disappearing
up ahead.

9

The Bridge

"Where'd you go this time?" Mia muttered, wiping sweat out of her eyes, as she peered up into the treetops.

She'd been following the white flashes for nearly an hour, and she still wasn't sure if it was a monkey up there or something else entirely. Glancing to her left, she saw the brighter light of the clearing just a short distance away through the trees. She couldn't see the gorge itself from where she was, but she was quite sure she'd retraced the whole way she'd travelled alongside it by now. Maybe even more.

The thought brought her worries back again. She noticed that the light was already changing as the sun headed for the horizon. It would set in about two hours, maybe less, and then what would Mia do?

"I'll set up camp by the gorge," she told herself aloud. "Maybe I can find enough dry wood to make a fire."

She chewed on her lower lip as she thought about that. Could she actually make a fire by rubbing two sticks together or something? She was pretty sure Olivia would know exactly how to do that – but Olivia wasn't here.

Stepping out into the clearing by the gorge, she saw that she'd been right. The scenery here didn't look familiar, which meant she'd walked further than she'd been before.

At least that means I'm closer to the bridge, even if it's still a couple of hours' walk away, she thought to herself, trying to look on the bright side – just like Emma would have done if she were in the same situation.

Mia glanced ahead. If she forgot about the white monkey and walked as fast as she could, maybe the big metal bridge would come into view before it got dark. Or maybe not.

"Hey, what's that?" she murmured, squinting at something hanging over the gorge just half a kilometre ahead.

She took a few steps towards it. Could it be . . . a bridge? She was sure the bridge she'd crossed on her scooter was still a good distance away. Besides, whatever was hanging there wasn't metal. But what was it?

With one last glance at the jungle, she hurried forward. *Yes*, she realized as she got closer. *It is another bridge!*

For a moment she felt hopeful. The camp was pretty much directly across from this part of the gorge, probably only about an hour's walk away. If she crossed this bridge, she could be back before nightfall!

Then she got closer, and her heart sank again. This bridge definitely wasn't anything like the sturdy metal structure further up the gorge. It was rickety and thin, made of wooden steps tied together by rope that appeared to be fraying at every knot.

"This one must have been abandoned when the new one was built," she murmured. "And no wonder!"

Mia was so disappointed she could hardly stand it. The idea of staying out here overnight seemed even worse now that she had seemed so close to reaching camp before dark.

Taking another step towards the bridge, she studied it carefully. The knots were frayed, but they looked sturdy. And while a few of the wooden steps were cracked or missing entirely, most of them were still in place. Maybe . . .

"No," she whispered with a shudder. Even Stephanie wouldn't be brave enough to cross a scary bridge like that. There was no way Mia could do it.

Could she?

Suddenly it all seemed like too much to think about. She was so close to safety, and

yet so, so far . . . Mia felt so sorry for herself
that she sat down and started to cry, burying
her face in her hands. She didn't even look
up when she heard something scurry past
her. Everything felt so hopeless that even the
prospect of seeing another interesting jungle
creature wasn't enough to distract her.

Then Mia heard a funny little screech
coming from – the gorge? She wiped her eyes
and looked up just in time to catch a flutter of
movement on the opposite side.

She gasped as something white and furry
scampered into the shelter of the trees.

"What?" she exclaimed, rubbing her eyes
and climbing to her feet. "How'd you get
over *there*?"

She stepped to the edge of the gorge by the
bridge, staring across at the trees. She must

have spotted the white monkey! She was sure of it this time – well, almost sure, anyway. But if it was on *that* side of the gorge now . . .

"Are you there?" called Mia, towards where she thought the monkey could be. "Did you cross the bridge while I wasn't looking? You rascal!"

Mia laughed despite the trouble she was in. All this time, she'd been trying like crazy to spot the white monkey and it seemed like it had sneaked right past her the one moment she wasn't looking! She couldn't wait to tell Andrea about it – she loved funny stories like that.

Mia's smile faded as she thought of something else. It looked like the monkey had just made it across the bridge. Did that mean Mia could make it across, too?

She felt uneasy as she studied the rough wooden boards again. They looked so narrow, so unstable. And the only things to hold onto were a pair of rough looking ropes on either side. If the boards were still damp and Mia slipped, or a strong wind blew . . .

Mia swallowed hard, trying not to imagine what could happen. Instead, she stuck one toe onto the first board, kicking at it to test it. The motion made the entire bridge sway.

"This is crazy," Mia whispered, glancing down into the gorge with a shudder. How did she know the white monkey had really crossed just now? What if it had been over there all along?

She backed away a few steps and felt her foot slip in a patch of mud. Glancing down, she gasped. There was a monkey paw print there – right at her end of the bridge!

"That wasn't there when I got here," she said aloud. "I would have seen it. Wouldn't I?"

She stepped closer to the bridge again. This time she reached out and grabbed one of the ropes on the side, then pressed down again on the first board with one foot. The bridge swayed a little, but the more weight she put on it, the steadier it felt. She yanked on the rope, and it held firm.

Could she do this? Mia stood still for a moment, frozen with fear.

Another screech came from across the way. Mia peered across. Was that a little white face looking back at her from the trees?

"Are you trying to tell me it's safe to cross?" she whispered, staring as hard as she could. But the face had already disappeared back into the leaves, so fast that Mia wasn't entirely sure she'd actually seen it.

Still, she couldn't help feeling a little braver. Clutching the rope handhold, she carefully leaned forward, and put her other foot on the bridge.

She held her breath, but . . . nothing happened. The bridge seemed strong enough to hold her. So she took another careful step, and then another. Before she knew it, she was several metres out.

This bridge looks scary, but I guess it's pretty safe after all, she thought, sliding her hands along the ropes as she took several more steps. *Kind of like zip lining, maybe.*

Thinking about that reminded Mia of her friends, which made her feel braver still. She could almost hear them cheering her on as she continued walking across, putting one foot in front of the other.

"Do you see anything?" Emma asked.

Stephanie shook her head, banking the helicopter into a broad sweeping turn. "Just trees," she said.

"Me too." Andrea sounded really sad. "Maybe we should go back and see if she came back, or if Matthew talked to the village again."

"I suppose you're right," Olivia sighed. "It will be dark soon anyway."

Stephanie nodded and turned back towards home. It felt as if they'd flown over the entire jungle, and they hadn't seen any sign of Mia. Where could she be? "We're coming to the gorge again," Emma commented as the helicopter sped along. "It looks different here, though."

"I think we're west of the bridge," Olivia said. "I've been trying to keep track of where we've gone."

Stephanie glanced at the instrument panel. "I think you're right. We should be about three or four kilometres west of where we crossed on the zip lines, which puts us pretty much due south of camp."

Andrea leaned closer to the window. "Wait, if we're that far from the bridge, what's that?"

Stephanie looked at where her friend was pointing. "Weird," she said. "It looks like another bridge." But she wasn't that interested. Her mind was racing, trying to work out a new plan to find Mia. Maybe if they took out the Jeep again, and a strong torch . . .

"Look! What's that?" Emma exclaimed as the gorge passed beneath them.

Stephanie blinked and glanced at her. "What's what?"

"I saw something back there by the bridge," Emma said. "Something white!"

Andrea jumped up and down in her seat. "Turn back, Steph," she exclaimed. "Maybe it was Mia!"

"It could have been." Olivia sounded hopeful. "Was she wearing a white shirt today?"

"I don't remember." Stephanie was already turning the helicopter around. "But we'd better go back and see!"

Soon they were over the gorge again. "It's her!" Andrea cried, her face pressed to the window. "I see her! There's someone on that bridge – it's got to be Mia!"

10

Rescued

Mia was so focused on getting across the rope bridge that it took a while for her to notice the whine of the helicopter approaching. As she reached the far side of the gorge, however, it became impossible to ignore. Just as her foot touched solid ground, the chopper settled to a landing less than fifty metres away.

"Mia!" Emma cried, flinging her door open and jumping out. "Thank goodness!"

Mia could hardly believe her eyes as Andrea, Olivia, and Stephanie jumped out, too.

"You found me!" she exclaimed, rushing towards her friends. "Thank you so much!"

Emma flung her arms around Mia, squeezing so tightly that Mia couldn't breathe. But she didn't mind. She laughed as the other three joined them, wrapping their arms around her in one huge friendly hug.

Finally everyone backed away to catch their breath. "Oh," Emma said, looking Mia up and down. "You're not wearing a white shirt."

Mia smiled as she glanced down at her khaki shorts and red T-shirt. "Trust you to think about fashion at a time like this!" she laughed.

But Olivia was frowning. "No, she's right." She glanced at Emma. "If it wasn't Mia's white clothes you saw, what was it?"

"Never mind," said Stephanie, smiling. "It made us turn around and find Mia, and that's what's important."

"What are you guys talking about?" Mia asked.

"We were heading back to camp when Emma saw something white down here," Andrea explained. "That's the only reason we came back."

Mia's eyes widened. "Something white?" she said. "Was it – could it have been a – a monkey?"

She quickly told the others what she'd seen. They listened quietly.

" . . . so I never really got a good look at it," she finished. "It could have been a grey langur, or maybe some other kind of monkey. I just have this funny feeling, though – I think it really was the white monkey. And that it showed me the way across the bridge." She shrugged and shot her friends a hopeful look. Would they think she was crazy?

But Andrea pulled her into another hug. "I believe you," she said. "You're our animal expert, right? If you think it was a white monkey, I bet you're right."

"Me too," Stephanie agreed, and Emma nodded and smiled.

Olivia still looked a little skeptical, but she shrugged. "Even the scientists say there are probably tons of undiscovered species out in the jungle. So who knows? Maybe you did

find a white monkey – and maybe it really did try to help you. There are all kinds of scientific studies about the connection between man and other primates."

"That's cool, Olivia," Stephanie laughed. "But why don't you tell us about it when we get back to camp, where we can finally sit down and rest!"

The thought of getting back to the rescue base made everyone smile. "Anyway," said Stephanie. "I believe you too, Mia."

"Thanks," Mia said, smiling at her friends. "Should we head back to camp now? I'm exhausted."

"Definitely!" Stephanie turned and hurried towards the helicopter. The others followed.

Mia hung back for a moment, gazing at the trees where she'd seen the white monkey. Or thought she had. Was it really out there somewhere?

The brush at the base of the trees rustled and parted. Mia gasped as a furry white creature stepped into view. It looked sort of like a grey langur, but not quite. It had a smaller, stouter body and a different shaped face – and pure white fur from the top of its head to the end of its long tail.

"The monkey!" Mia blurted out in amazement just as the monkey leaped back into the jungle with a flick of its tail.

Her friends spun around. "Really?" Andrea cried.

"Where?" Stephanie exclaimed.

"Too late," Mia said. "It's gone."

She was disappointed, but she still couldn't stop smiling. She'd seen the white monkey, and that was enough – for now, at least. Maybe someday she'd try to find it again so her friends could see it too. But for now just knowing it really was out there was enough.

"Come on," said Mia happily, heading for the helicopter with a huge smile. "I've had plenty of adventure for one day. Let's get back to camp!"

THE END

Jungle Photo Album

Trekking through the jungle isn't all fun and games!
As well as getting lost, Mia also had to find her way
past some scary wildlife, sticky spiderwebs, slippery
mud trails and rickety bridges! Here are some photos
from her jungle adventure.

Monkey Business

Did you know that gorillas, chimpanzees, orangutans, and gibbons are actually not monkeys, but apes? Apes don't have tails to help them swing through the trees, so they'll usually stay comfortably on the ground, while monkeys perform acrobatics in the treetops!

Check out these fun facts about some very interesting monkey species:

Gray langur: Mia and her friends see these monkeys near the Jungle Camp. Gray langurs have gray fur and dark faces and ears. They are a very widespread species that have adapted to live in a variety of habitats, from the jungle to the city and everywhere in between.

Mandrill: Mandrills are not only the world's largest monkeys — they're also the most colourful, with red, blue, yellow, and white on their faces and other body parts. A group of mandrills is known as a 'horde'.

Pygmy marmoset: The pygmy marmoset is the smallest species of monkey, weighing just over 100 grams. It can rotate its head 180 degrees and eats mostly tree gum, though it also a enjoys a tasty insect or piece of fruit.

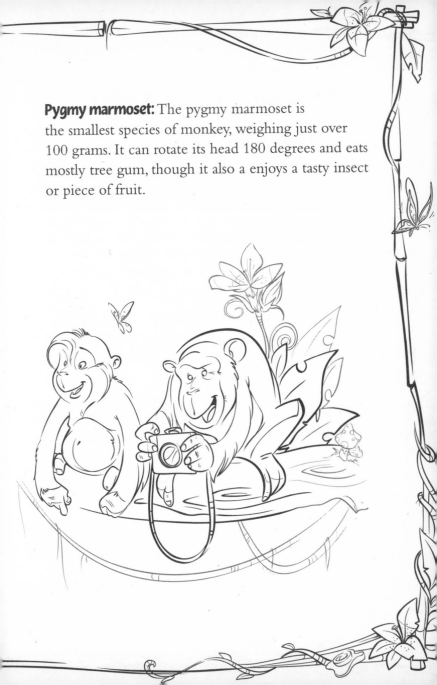

It's a Jungle Out There!

The jungle is a fascinating place, but it can be dangerous if you're not careful. Take this quiz to find out whether you know the best ways to stay safe during your outing.

1. You're enjoying a fun jungle hike when you take a wrong turn and lose the trail. Oh, no – you're lost! How would you react?

   a) I'd panic!
   b) I'd look for my footprints and try to follow them to find the trail.

2. What clothes would you wear in the jungle?

   a) I'd choose comfortable clothes and some protection from mosquitoes.
   b) I wouldn't go anywhere without my handbag!

3. What snacks would you pack in your bag for a jungle adventure?

   a) I'd take some energy bars with me.
   b) I wouldn't need any snacks. The jungle would provide all the food I would need!

Answers:

1. b Panicking never does anybody any good!

2. a It's not a good idea to take a handbag on a jungle adventure. You can lose it easily among the vast wildlife. Go for a comfy pack where you can put all the necessities.

3. a Try not to depend too much on the food from the jungle. While bananas or mangos may be quite safe to eat, you can never be sure that the fruit you've found is not poisonous.

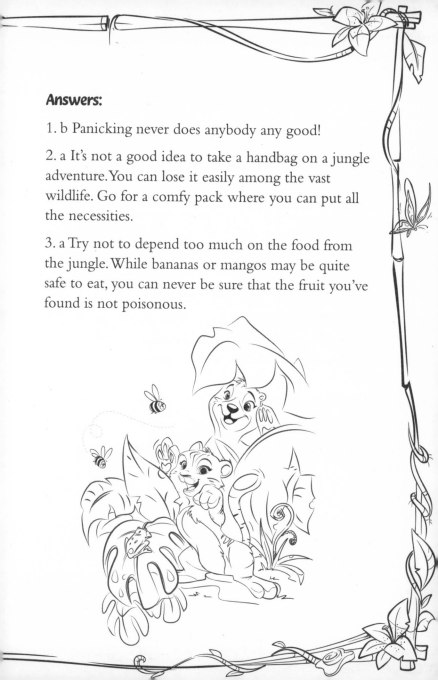

Travelling Companions

The LEGO® Friends love travelling together – but each girl has a different idea of the perfect vacation! Which Friend shares YOUR tastes?

If you like:

♥ Ancient buildings
♥ Prehistoric cultures
♥ Learning about different people

You and **STEPHANIE** would both love spending the day at an archeological site or museum. Stephanie especially loves the Archeological Mission near the Jungle Camp!

If you like:

♥ Taking care of animals
♥ Helping to grow interesting plants
♥ Exploring nature

You and **MIA** share a love of outdoorsy adventures, nature hikes, and other activities in which you can interact with the natural world. One of Mia's favourite places is the Jungle Quest site, where she helps the scientists seek out new species.

If you like:

♥ Extreme sports
♥ Sleeping under the stars
♥ Orienteering

You're probably a fan of adventures that use both brain and body, just like **OLIVIA**! She's always willing to go on a Survival Quest to test her skills and have a blast!

If you like:

♥ Beautiful things
♥ Socializing in the great outdoors
♥ Eating yummy food with good friends

You have a lot in common with **EMMA**, who loves organizing picnics and decorating her campsite with all the lovely flowers, leaves, and fruits she finds in the jungle. She sees just as much beauty in nature as she does at the art museum in Heartlake City.

If you like:

♥ Music
♥ Camping with friends
♥ Being creative

Guess what? You're a lot like **ANDREA**! She's always in the mood for a song – even if it's birdsong! Listening to the sounds of nature always inspires her to write songs she can perform around the campfire for her friends or back home at the Café.

Endangered Species

Mia, her friends, and the scientists and vets at the Jungle Camp are all concerned about endangered species. Are you? If so, here are a few interesting animals that are in danger of extinction.

Tigers are one of the easiest animals to recognize. However, they are also one of the most endangered due to illegal hunting (poaching) and loss of habitat.

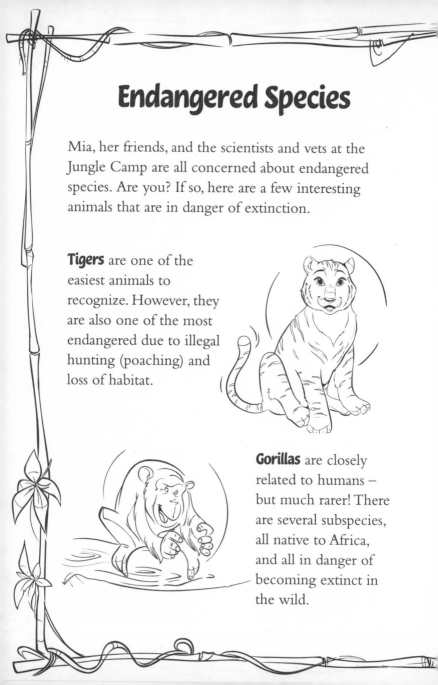

Gorillas are closely related to humans – but much rarer! There are several subspecies, all native to Africa, and all in danger of becoming extinct in the wild.

The blue whale is the largest animal in the world. It was hunted nearly to extinction in 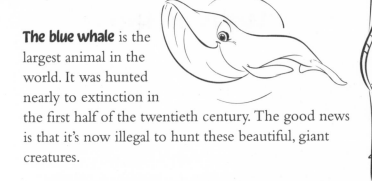 the first half of the twentieth century. The good news is that it's now illegal to hunt these beautiful, giant creatures.

The leatherback sea turtle is the largest living turtle with one of the smallest populations. Their numbers are declining due to humans damaging large numbers of turtle eggs, as well as pollution and other issues.

The giant panda is a popular attraction in zoos all over the world. However, its population in the wild is endangered because of habitat loss and a low natural birthrate.

Ways to Help

Mia and all of her friends are concerned about saving animals and protecting nature. If you're concerned about those things too, here are some things you can do to help:

♥ Visit a nearby national park or nature reserve. You can learn a lot about current issues and ways to get involved.

♥ Act locally. Join any local organizations you can find, put up a birdfeeder to help feed the neighborhood birds, or volunteer your time to help clean up trash or keep local hiking trails clear and safe.

♥ Check with the nearest zoo (or online) about virtually adopting an animal. This provides funds not only for that animal, but for other conservation projects as well.

♥ Reduce, Reuse, and Recycle. It really does help the environment – where both people and animals live!

♥ Share your knowledge. Talk to friends and family about what you're learning and doing. Maybe they'll want to help, too!